THE GRAPHIC NOVEL
William Shakespeare

QUICK TEXT VERSION

Script Adaptation: John McDonald
Character Designs & Original Artwork: Jon Haward
Colouring & Lettering: Nigel Dobbyn
Inking Assistant: Gary Erskine

Design & Layout: Jo Wheeler
Additional Information: Karen Wenborn

Editor in Chief: Clive Bryant

Macbeth: The Graphic Novel
Quick Text Version

William Shakespeare

First published: February 2008
Reprinted: July 2009, March 2012, February 2015

Published by: Classical Comics Ltd

Acknowledgments: Every effort has been made to trace copyright holders of
material reproduced in this book. Any rights not acknowledged here will be
acknowledged in subsequent editions if notice is given to Classical Comics Ltd.

Images on pages 3 & 6 reproduced with the kind permission of
the Trustees of the National Library of Scotland. © National Library of Scotland.

All enquiries should be addressed to:
Classical Comics Ltd.
PO Box 16310
Birmingham
B30 9EL
United Kingdom

info@classicalcomics.com
www.classicalcomics.com

ISBN: 978-1-906332-05-1

This book is printed by Graphy Cems, Spain using environmentally safe inks, on paper
from responsible sources. This material can be disposed of by recycling,
incineration for energy recovery, composting and biodegradation.

The rights of John McDonald, Jon Haward, Nigel Dobbyn and Gary Erskine
to be identified as the artists of this work have been asserted in accordance with
the Copyright, Designs and Patents Act 1988 sections 77 and 78.

Contents

✠━ ━✠

✠━ ━✠

Dramatis Personæ

Duncan
King of Scotland

Malcolm
Son of Duncan

Donalbain
Son of Duncan

Macduff
Nobleman of Scotland

Lenox
Nobleman of Scotland

Rosse
Nobleman of Scotland

Lady Macbeth
Wife of Macbeth

Lady Macduff
Wife of Macduff

Siward *Earl of Northumberland,
General of the English forces*

A Gentlewoman attending
to Lady Macbeth

Seyton
An officer attending to Macbeth

An English Doctor

A Scottish Doctor

A Porter

An Old Man

Murderer 1

Murderer 2

Murderer 3

Dramatis Personæ

Macbeth
General in the King's Army

Banquo
General in the King's Army

The Ghost of Banquo

Menteth
Nobleman of Scotland

Angus
Nobleman of Scotland

Cathness
Nobleman of Scotland

Young Siward
Son of Siward

Fleance
Son of Banquo

Boy
Son of Macduff

Witch 1

Witch 2

Witch 3

Hecate
The "Queen" Witch

and Lords, Ladies,
Officers, Soldiers,
Messengers, Attendants
and Apparitions.

Prologue

Scotland in the year 1040.

King Duncan has ruled the land for six years, ever since the death of his grandfather, Malcolm II. Duncan is a good king, but even under his kind and gentle ruling, Scotland is far from being a settled nation.

For centuries, following the departure of the Romans, the land has been split in two – with bands of Vikings in the north, and tribes of Saxons in the south. It's a barbaric land. Each local tribe has its own strong leader: men relying on the strength of their sword arm for honours and often having to fight for their very survival.

But the country is changing. With the reign of King Duncan came a rare promise of unity amongst the tribes to create a single, Scottish nation ruled by a single Scottish King. However, not everyone welcomes this peace. Some chieftains want to maintain their independence and continue to rebel against the King, often joining forces with warriors from other tribes and from other countries such as Ireland and Norway; and there are even some chieftains who would like to claim the title of King of Scotland for themselves.

To defend his crown, and to maintain order in his land, King Duncan commands a powerful army, led by noblemen who are experienced in the ways of war - and the mightiest and most trusted of these noblemen is King Duncan's cousin, the Thane of Glamis, otherwise known as…

…Macbeth.

Act One
Scene One

A deserted, open place...

CRAAACKKK!!!

WHEN SHALL WE MEET AGAIN? IN THUNDER OR IN RAIN?

WHEN THE BATTLE'S LOST AND WON.

BEFORE THE SETTING OF THE SUN.

WHERE?

ON THE HEATH.

TO MEET WITH MACBETH.

FAIR IS FOUL AND FOUL IS FAIR.

HOVER THROUGH THE FILTHY AIR.

FROM *FIFE*, WHERE THE NORWEGIANS HAVE BEEN ATTACKING, WITH THE HELP OF THE *THANE OF CAWDOR*.

BUT *MACBETH* FOUGHT THE NORWEGIAN KING *SINGLE-HANDEDLY* AND *BEAT* HIM.

GREAT NEWS!

THE NORWEGIANS HAVE NOW *SURRENDERED!*

HAVE THE THANE OF CAWDOR *EXECUTED* IMMEDIATELY, AND GIVE HIS *TITLE* TO *MACBETH*.

AS YOU WISH.

HIS *LOSS* IS MACBETH'S *GAIN*.

AND THANE OF CAWDOR.

SO THEY SAID.

WHO'S THIS?

THE KING IS *DELIGHTED* BY THE NEWS OF YOUR *VICTORY*, MACBETH.

WE'VE BEEN SENT TO ESCORT YOU *BACK* TO HIM.

HE'S DECIDED TO MAKE YOU *THANE OF CAWDOR.*

WHAT? DID THE WITCHES TELL THE *TRUTH?*

BUT THE THANE STILL *LIVES.*

NOT FOR LONG. HE IS TO BE *EXECUTED.*

CAN THIS BE TRUE?

THANK YOU.

NOW, LET'S GO TO *INVERNESS*, AND VISIT YOUR *CASTLE*.

I'LL GO ON AHEAD, TO TELL MY *WIFE*.

MALCOLM COULD BE A *PROBLEM*. IT'S A GOOD THING NOBODY CAN SEE WHAT I'M *THINKING* RIGHT NOW.

LET'S QUICKLY *FOLLOW* MACBETH TO HIS *CASTLE*.

Act One Scene Five

At Macbeth's castle, in Inverness, Lady Macbeth receives news from her husband...

"THREE *WITCHES* TOLD ME I'D BE THANE OF CAWDOR, THEN I WAS *MADE* THANE OF CAWDOR."

"THEY ALSO TOLD ME I'D BE *KING*! THEN THEY *VANISHED*. I HAD TO *TELL* YOU, STRAIGHT AWAY."

YOU'RE THANE OF GLAMIS AND CAWDOR! AND YOU *WILL* BE KING. BUT, YOU'RE TOO *NOBLE* TO DO WHAT NEEDS TO BE DONE.

I KNOW YOU *WANT* TO BE KING, BUT YOU'LL ONLY GET WHAT YOU WANT BY *TAKING* IT.

COME HOME. I'LL MAKE SURE *NOTHING* GETS IN THE WAY OF OUR GOLDEN FUTURE.

MACBETH! MY WORTHY THANE! YOUR LETTER HAS MADE ME SO *HAPPY...*

DUNCAN WILL BE HERE TONIGHT, MY LOVE.

AND WHEN IS HE LEAVING?

TOMORROW.

HE WON'T LIVE TO *SEE* TOMORROW! DON'T LOOK SO *GUILTY* -- *WELCOME* HIM AND LOOK *INNOCENT...*

...BUT BE READY TO *KILL* HIM. LEAVE THE DETAILS TO *ME.*

WE'LL TALK LATER.

THIS IS OUR *CHANCE.* LEAVE IT TO ME.

Act Two
Scene Two

A while later...

THE WINE THAT HAS MADE THEM *DRUNK* HAS MADE ME *BRAVE* -- AND MACBETH IS *KILLING* THE KING RIGHT NOW.

WHO'S THERE?

OH *NO!* WE'VE BEEN *DISCOVERED!* I LEFT THE DAGGERS *READY* FOR HIM - HE *COULDN'T* HAVE *MISSED* THEM.

MY HUSBAND!

IT'S *DONE.*

34

STOP ACTING LIKE A *FOOL* AND WASH THAT *BLOOD* OFF YOUR HANDS.

TAKE THOSE *DAGGERS* BACK AND SMEAR THE *GUARDS* WITH HIS *BLOOD.*

SLAAAP!!!

I'M NOT GOING BACK THERE!

WEAKLING! I'LL DO IT!

BANG! BANG!

EVERY LITTLE *NOISE* FRIGHTENS ME --

AND *ALL THE WATERS OF THE OCEANS* WON'T WASH THE *BLOOD* OFF THESE HANDS.

41

43

DO THEY *KNOW* WHO MURDERED THE *KING?*

THE ONES *MACBETH* KILLED.

AND *WHY?*

FOR *MONEY.* ODDLY, THE *KING'S SONS* HAVE ALSO *RUN AWAY.* THEY COULD HAVE BEEN *INVOLVED.*

THEY WOULDN'T *KILL* THEIR *OWN FATHER.* I SUPPOSE THAT *MACBETH* WILL BE MADE *KING?*

HE'S ALREADY GONE TO *SCONE* TO BE *CROWNED.*

ARE *YOU* GOING TO *SCONE?*

NO, I'M GOING HOME TO *FIFE.*

Act Three Scene One

Macbeth is now King of Scotland. In the King's Palace at Forres, Banquo is suspicious...

TAN-TARA! TAN-TARA!

AH, OUR *CHIEF GUEST* IS HERE.

IT WOULDN'T BE THE SAME *WITHOUT* HIM.

YOU HAVE IT *ALL* NOW! JUST AS THE *WITCHES* PROMISED. BUT I THINK YOU'VE PLAYED *DIRTY* TO *GET* IT.

STILL, THE *PROPHECY* MAY COME TRUE FOR *ME*, TOO.

WE'RE HAVING A *BANQUET* TONIGHT AND WE'D LIKE *YOU* TO *BE* THERE.

OF COURSE.

49

51

IF *THAT'S* SO, THEN IT'S ALL BEEN FOR *NOTHING.* HIS *FAMILY* WILL TAKE EVERYTHING *AWAY* FROM ME.

THUMP!!!

I'VE MURDERED DUNCAN FOR *THEM!* GIVEN MY SOUL TO THE DEVIL TO MAKE *THEM* KINGS! I CAN'T LET THAT HAPPEN.

WHO'S THERE?

WAIT OUTSIDE THE DOOR.

WAS IT *YESTERDAY* WE SPOKE?

YES, YOUR HIGHNESS.

54

Elsewhere in the King's Palace...

HAS *BANQUO* GONE FROM THE PALACE?

YES, MADAM. BUT HE'S COMING BACK *TONIGHT.*

TELL THE KING I'D LIKE A *WORD.*

YES, MADAM.

WHAT *GOOD* IS ANYTHING IF IT DOESN'T BRING *HAPPINESS?* BETTER TO BE *DEAD* THAN TO LIVE IN A *WAKING NIGHTMARE.*

HOW ARE YOU, MY LORD? WHY ARE YOU HIDING AWAY, *BROODING* OVER WHAT YOU *CANNOT CHANGE?*

THE *JOB'S* ONLY *HALF DONE.*

WE'RE STILL IN *DANGER.*

I *WON'T* GIVE IN TO THE *NIGHTMARE* THAT OUR LIVES HAVE BECOME! I'D RATHER BE *DEAD.*

56

61

67

I'M GOING TO FIND THE *WITCHES* TOMORROW.

I NEED TO KNOW WHAT TO *DO.* THERE'S SO MUCH *BLOOD* ON MY HANDS THAT *MORE* MURDER WON'T *MATTER* ALL THAT MUCH.

YOU NEED TO *SLEEP.*

LET'S GO TO BED.

81

95

MACDUFF! YOU'VE *CONVINCED* ME. MACBETH'S TRIED TO *TRICK* ME BEFORE, SO I HAD TO *TEST* YOU.

FORGET WHAT I JUST SAID, I'M NOT LIKE THAT AT ALL.

BEFORE YOU ARRIVED, I WAS READY TO SET OUT FOR SCOTLAND WITH AN *ARMY* OF *TEN THOUSAND MEN.*

NOW WE CAN LEAD THEM *TOGETHER!*

PLEASE *SAY* SOMETHING.

I'M *CONFUSED.* IS THIS THE *TRUTH?*

YOU'LL SEE...

An English doctor approaches...

WHERE IS THE *KING?*

HE'S SEEING TO THE *SICK PEOPLE. GOD* GAVE HIM THE POWER TO *HEAL* THEIR *DISEASE.*

Late at night in Dunsinane Castle...

NOTHING FOR **TWO NIGHTS** - I'M STARTING TO **DOUBT** YOUR **STORY.**

SINCE THE **KING** WENT TO **WAR,** I HAVE SEEN HER **GET OUT OF BED** AND SLEEPWALK.

DOES SHE **SAY** ANYTHING?

NOTHING I CAN **REPEAT.**

YOU CAN TELL **ME.**

NO SIR, I'LL TELL **NO ONE.**

HERE SHE COMES NOW.

See? She's *fast* asleep.

105

Did you *hear* that?

THE THANE OF FIFE HAD A *WIFE:* WHERE IS SHE *NOW?*

WILL THESE HANDS NEVER BE CLEAN?

DON'T LOSE YOUR *NERVE,* MY LORD, OR YOU'LL RUIN *EVERYTHING.*

You have *seen* things you *shouldn't* have.

And she has *said* things she shouldn't have, *too.*

I CAN STILL SMELL *BLOOD.* ALL THE *PERFUME* IN THE *WORLD* WON'T TAKE IT AWAY.

OOOHHH!!!

She's very *troubled.*

I don't *envy* her.

Will she be all right?

I can't *say* for sure.

WASH YOUR HANDS! DON'T LOOK SO FRIGHTENED. BANQUO'S DEAD - HE CAN'T COME OUT OF HIS GRAVE.

Not that TOO?

LET'S GO TO BED. THERE'S SOMEONE KNOCKING AT THE GATE.

WHAT'S DONE CANNOT BE UNDONE.

WILL SHE GO BACK TO BED NOW?

YES.

THERE ARE MANY RUMOURS GOING AROUND. I THINK SHE NEEDS A PRIEST, NOT A DOCTOR.

LOOK AFTER HER. MAKE SURE SHE COMES TO NO HARM. I DARE NOT SAY WHAT I'M THINKING.

GOODNIGHT, DOCTOR.

The Scottish countryside, near Dunsinane...

THE *ENGLISH FORCES* ARE *CLOSE,* LED BY *MALCOLM, MACDUFF* AND *OLD SIWARD.*

WE'LL MEET THEM NEAR *BIRNAM WOOD.*

IS *DONALBAIN* WITH THEM?

NO, BUT *SIWARD'S SON* IS.

WHAT'S *MACBETH* DOING?

HE'S AT *DUNSINANE. SOME* SAY HE'S GONE *MAD.*

HIS *SECRET MURDERS* ARE COMING BACK TO *HAUNT* HIM. HIS *MEN* ARE *DESERTING* HIM, AND HIS *KINGSHIP* IS *USELESS* TO HIM NOW.

CURE HER! CAN'T YOU HEAL A SICK MIND?

ONLY *SHE* CAN DO THAT FOR *HERSELF.*

TO *HELL* WITH YOUR MEDICINE, THEN!

PUT ON MY *ARMOUR!*

SEYTON, SEND OUT THE HORSEMEN!

THE *THANES* ARE *DESERTING* ME.

SEND THEM OUT!

Act Five
Scene Five

Dunsinane Castle –
Macbeth prepares
for battle...

HANG OUT OUR *FLAGS.*

THEY'RE *COMING,* BUT WE WILL *HOLD THEM OFF.*

IF THEY HADN'T BEEN JOINED BY THE ONES WHO *DESERTED* ME, WE'D HAVE MET THEM *FACE TO FACE* ON THE *BATTLEFIELD.*

SCREEEAAAMMM!!

WHAT WAS *THAT?*

WOMEN SCREAMING, MY LORD.

117

A *SCREAM* LIKE THAT USED TO MAKE ME *SHUDDER.* BUT I'VE SEEN *SO MUCH HORROR* LATELY, THAT *NOTHING* BOTHERS ME NOW.

WHAT *WAS* IT?

THE *QUEEN...* IS *DEAD,* MY LORD.

SHE SHOULD HAVE DIED *ANOTHER* TIME. A *BETTER* TIME.

TOMORROW... THE *NEXT* DAY... THE DAY *AFTER.* WHAT DOES IT *MATTER?*

HER BRIEF *CANDLELIGHT* HAS *BLOWN OUT.*

LIFE IS JUST A *SHADOW.* IT'S A STORY TOLD BY A *FOOL,* FULL OF *NOISE...* BUT MEANING *NOTHING.*

118

123

I WISH THE MEN WE *LOST* WERE STILL HERE.

SOME HAD TO DIE. WE DIDN'T LOSE *MANY.*

MACDUFF IS MISSING... AND SO IS YOUR *SON.*

YOUR *SON* WAS *KILLED*, MY LORD. BUT HE *DIED* LIKE A *MAN.*

THEN... HE'S *DEAD?*

YES – AND CARRIED OFF THE BATTLEFIELD.

WERE HIS *WOUNDS* ON THE *FRONT* OF HIS BODY?

YES.

Macbeth

End

William Shakespeare

(c.1564 - 1616 AD)

William Shakespeare is one of the most widely read authors and possibly the best dramatist ever to live. The actual date of his birth is not known, but traditionally April 23rd 1564 (St George's Day) has been his accepted birthday, as this was three days before his baptism. He died on the same date in 1616, aged fifty-two.

The life of William Shakespeare can be divided into three acts. The first twenty years of his life were spent in Stratford-upon-Avon where he grew up, went to school, got married and became a father. The next twenty-five years he spent as an actor and playwright in London; and he spent his last few years back in Stratford-upon-Avon, where he enjoyed his retirement in moderate wealth gained from his successful years in the theatre.

William was the eldest son of tradesman John Shakespeare and Mary Arden, and the third of eight children. His father was later elected mayor of Stratford, which was the highest post a man in civic politics could attain. In sixteenth-century England, William was lucky to survive into adulthood; syphilis, scurvy, smallpox, tuberculosis, typhus and dysentery shortened life expectancy at the time to approximately thirty-five years. The Bubonic Plague took the lives of many and was believed to have been the cause of death for three of William's seven siblings.

Little is known of William's childhood, other than it is thought that he attended the local grammar school, where he studied Latin and English Literature. In 1582, at the age of eighteen, William married a local farmer's daughter, Anne Hathaway, who was eight years his senior and three months pregnant. During their marriage they had three children: Susanna, born on May 26th 1583 and twins, Hamnet and Judith, born on February 2nd 1585. Hamnet, William's only son, caught Bubonic Plague and died aged just eleven.

Five years into his marriage, in 1587, William's wife and children stayed in Stratford, while he moved to London. He appeared as an actor at 'The Theatre' (England's first permanent theatre) and gave public recitals of his own poems; but he soon became famous for his playwriting. His fame soon spread far and wide. When Queen Elizabeth I died in 1603, the new King James I (who was already King James VI of Scotland) gave royal consent for Shakespeare's acting company, "The Lord Chamberlain's Men" to be called "The King's Men" in return for entertaining the court. This association was to shape a number of plays, such as *Macbeth*, which was written to please the Scottish King.

In just twenty-three years, between 1590 and 1613, William Shakespeare is attributed with writing thirty-eight plays, one-hundred-and-fifty-four sonnets and five poems. No original manuscript exists for any of his plays, so it is hard to accurately date them. However, from their contents and reports of the day it is believed that his first play was *The Taming of the Shrew* and that his last completed work was *Two Noble Kinsmen*, written two years before he died. The cause of his death remains unknown.

He was buried on April 25th 1616, two days after his death, at the Church of the Holy Trinity (the same Church where he had been baptised fifty-two years earlier). His gravestone bears these words, believed to have been written by William himself:-

"Good friend for Jesus sake forbear,
To dig the dust enclosed here!
Blest be the man that spares these stones,
And curst be he that moves my bones"

At the time of his death, William had substantial properties, which he bestowed on his family and associates from the theatre. Most went to his eldest daughter, Susanna. Curiously, all he left to his wife Anne was his second best bed!

William Shakespeare's last direct descendant died in 1670. She was his granddaughter, Elizabeth.

The Real Macbeth

(c.1005 - 1057 AD)

Macbeth is one of Shakespeare's most famous characters. It is a name that's known the whole world over; but many people don't realise that the story is linked to actual historical events – even though those events have been heavily embellished and altered for the sake of entertainment.

Shakespeare obtained his information about the real Macbeth from Raphael Holinshed's book, *The Chronicles of England, Scotland and Ireland*, published in 1574 (which Shakespeare used as a primary resource for all of his historical plays). Holinshed himself derived his information from a variety of sources, most notably Andrew of Wyntoun's *Orygynale Cronykil* ("Original Chronicle") which traces a history of Scotland from Biblical times, and Hector Boece's

Scotorum Historiae ("Scottish History"), published in 1526 and translated from Latin into English by John Bellenden in 1535.

Macbeth, or rather Mac Bethad as he would have been called, was King of Scotland from 1040 to 1057 (although in Shakespeare's play, his reign is made to appear significantly less than seventeen years). The name "Mac Bethad" means

"son of life", and is actually Irish, rather than Scottish in origin.

Eleventh century Scotland was a barbaric land; with war and ruthless slaughter being a fact of life. Survival depended on having a strong and capable local ruler or chieftain to protect both life and property. Such a leader would provide a strong paternalistic rule, guarding the family, community and land from all enemies.

Some of these enemies could be, and often were, collections of distant family members challenging the current leadership.

A number of local rulers would often unite under the nominal leadership of one "king" to promote their common interests and to wage war on other more distant clans. Interestingly, in those times, kings and rulers could name their own successor — it wasn't a privilege that was handed down from parent to eldest child as the monarchy operates today. However, family linkage tended to be respected and the title usually passed to a relative of the king — selected as being the one most suitable for immediate rule, and not necessarily the natural heir. Understandably, this selection process would have been challenged, especially by those individuals who felt that they had a greater right to become king than the person taking on the title. Such grievances were often dealt with or pre-empted by the murdering of family members judged unsuitable for power, to ensure that the "favourite" won the race.

Macbeth was the son of Findláech mac Ruaidrí (who was a High Steward of Moray) in the north of Scotland, around 1005. His mother's name is unknown, and indeed her own parentage is inaccurately recorded. It is uncertain whether she was the daughter of King

Kenneth II or of King Malcolm II. However, that is largely immaterial as whichever man was Macbeth's grandfather, would be a strong enough family link for him to make a claim for the throne.

In 1020, Macbeth's father Findláech died. It is thought that he was killed, most probably by his brother Máel Brigté's son Máel Coluim (Malcolm). Findláech's title of High Steward went to his nephew Gille Coemgáin. In 1032, Gille Coemgáin and fifty other people were burned to death as punishment for the murder of Findláech. This act of retribution could well have been carried out by

Macbeth and his allies. Following Gille Coemgáin's death, Macbeth took the title of High Steward of Moray.

It was around this time that he married Gille Coemgáin's widow, Gruoch, and became step-father to her son, Lulach (which explains why Shakespeare has Lady Macbeth talk about motherhood, whereas at no time does Macbeth make any reference to being a father. Moreover, Macduff states that Macbeth has no children in Act IV Scene III (page 102)). Macbeth's marriage to Gruoch was significant, because she was the grand-daughter of Kenneth III. Therefore through their combined ancestors the marriage ensured that Macbeth had a strong claim to the throne.

Within a very short space of time, Macbeth's rival Gille Coemgáin had not only lost his life, but his title and his widowed wife had gone swiftly to Macbeth.

While Macbeth was a high-ranking lord of Moray, the King at the time was Donnchad mac Crináin (King Duncan I). Duncan succeeded to the throne when his grandfather, King Malcolm II died at Glamis. It is thought likely that Malcolm had engineered the position of Duncan taking over from him, through the tactical assassination of any family members who might feel they had a stronger claim to the crown.

Given the circumstances, it would have been a sensible course of action for Duncan to make peace with his remaining family, in particular his cousin Thorfinn the Mighty (Earl of Orkney), his cousin Macbeth, and the person closest to his throne in terms of lineage, namely Gruoch, the wife of Macbeth. Duncan appears to have been unsuccessful in uniting the "royal family", and Macbeth pressed his own claim to the throne with the help of that same cousin and ally, Earl Thorfinn of Orkney. He eventually won the crown by slaying Duncan at Bothgowanan near Elgin in 1040.

Macbeth has been judged by history to be a more able king than his predecessor. Under his rule the kingdom became relatively stable and reasonably prosperous, so much so, that by 1050 he was confident enough to leave the country for a number of months and make a pilgrimage to Rome. At this time he was said to have been so wealthy that he "scattered alms like seed corn". As Wyntoun's *Orygynale Cronykil* says:-

"In pilgrimage þidder he come,
And in almus he sew siluer"

All was not peaceful, however, and in 1054 Duncan I's son, Máel Coluim mac Donnchada (Malcolm Canmore, nicknamed "big head"), challenged Macbeth for the throne of Scotland. He did so in alliance with Siward, Earl of Northumbria (who also happened to be the cousin of Duncan's widow) and they took control of much of southern Scotland. Three years later, on 15 August 1057 Macbeth's army was finally defeated at the Battle of Lumphanan, in Aberdeenshire. Macbeth was killed in battle. He is believed to be buried in the graveyard at Saint Oran's Chapel on the Isle of Iona, the last of many Kings of Alba and Dalriada to be laid to rest there. This site is also supposed to be the final resting place of King Duncan I.

Unlike in Shakespeare's play, the killing of Macbeth didn't result in the crown going straight to Duncan's son Malcolm. It first went to Macbeth's step-son Lulach, on the basis that Kenneth III was his maternal great-grandfather. Lulach was a weak king and ridiculed, being called "Lulach the Simple" or "Lulach the Fool". After a few months of rule, he was murdered; and Malcolm, son of Duncan I, became King Malcolm III of Scotland.

No-one knows what happened to Lady Macbeth. Dramatically, Shakespeare has her losing her sanity and taking her own life — however there is no record of that happening, or even of her falling to a bloody death. Having lived through the murder of her first husband, the killing of her second husband in battle, and the murder of her son, even if she was to outlive them all, it's unlikely that she enjoyed any form of happiness.

Macbeth and the Kings of Scotland

Key:
Parent of ——————
Married ══════════

"Malcolm I"
King 943-954
Máel Coluim mac Domnaill

"Duff"
King 962-966
Duib mac Máel Coluim

"Kenneth II"
King 971-995
Cináeda mac Máel Coluim

Domnall

"Kenneth III"
King 997-1005
Cináeda mac Duib

"Malcolm II"
King 1005-1034
Máel Coluim mac Cináeda

Ruadri

First wife - name unknown | 1 | Boite mac Cináeda | 2 | Gruoch

Máel Brigté

Mormaer of Moray
Findláech mac Ruaidrí

Donada

Bethoc (eldest)

Máel Coluim

Gille Coemgáin | 1 | "Lady Macbeth" Gruoch ingen Boite | 2 | "Macbeth" King 1040-1057 Mac Bethad

"Duncan I"
King 1034-1040
Donnchad mac Crináin

Suthen

Lulach
King 1057-1058
"The Fool"

"Malcolm III"
King 1058-1093
Máel Coluim mac Donnchada

"Donald III"
King 1093-1097
Domnall Bán

The Macbeth Murder Trail

1020 – Macbeth's father Findláech died – thought to have been killed by his own nephew, Máel Coluim. His title of High Steward went to Máel Coluim's brother, Gille Coemgáin.

1032 – Gille Coemgáin and 50 other people were burned to death as punishment for the killing of Findláech. Thought to have been carried out by Macbeth and his allies as retribution for killing his father. Macbeth takes his title (that had been his father's) and also takes Gille Coemgáin's widow, Gruoch, for his wife.

There is another theory, that Gille Coemgáin killed Boite mac Cináeda because he had made his wife the heiress to his estate. As retaliation for this murder, Boite's wife

Gruoch (the stepmother of the Gruoch that married Gille Coemgáin and later Macbeth) mustered an army to kill Gille Coemgáin.

1040 – Macbeth killed King Duncan I at Bothgowanan.

1050 – Macbeth went on a pilgrimage to Rome.

1054 – Máel Coluim mac Donnchada (Malcolm, son of King Duncan I) stakes his claim to the throne and challenges Macbeth in the first of a series of battles.

1057 – Macbeth's army is finally defeated by Malcolm's army at the Battle of Lumphanan. Macbeth is killed in battle. Macbeth's step-son Lulach becomes King.

1057 – After only a few months of rule, Malcolm kills Lulach and becomes King Malcolm III of Scotland.

The History of Shakespeare's Macbeth

When comparing the play to the actual historical events, it is clear that those events were merely inspiration for Shakespeare's own take on the story. It is unlikely that he deliberately intended to misrepresent the facts; however it is important to recognise that as a playwright, Shakespeare had a responsibility to entertain his audience with his works. Therefore, what takes place on the stage is an artistic modification of what took place in history; to give the best portrayal of the plots and motives of the characters in order to arrive at a worthy spectacle. Amongst other things, Shakespeare possessed good business sense — and a successful play would draw in the fee-paying public to provide him and his troupe with an income.

But money was not his sole concern. His position in society was paramount, and of prime importance was the need to pander to the monarch.

Macbeth is thought to have been written to be performed in honour of a royal visit by the King of Denmark to King James I in 1606. King James I became King of England in 1603 when Elizabeth I died. He was already King of Scotland (King James VI of Scotland). Interestingly, James I was a keen scholar, and had a deep interest in witchcraft; so much so that in 1597 he wrote a book on the subject which he called *Daemonologie* and in it he advocated that witches should be dealt with severely. In addition, he was a keen supporter of the arts, having the title of "The King's Men" bestowed upon Shakespeare's acting company soon after his coronation. In return, The King's Men were expected to perform at court whenever they were asked, which amounted to around a dozen performances each year.

Setting the play in Scotland and including elements of witchcraft appears to be a deliberate attempt by Shakespeare to please the new King. But he can't take the credit for including witchcraft in the tale of *Macbeth*: we have Holinshed to thank for that. Raphael Holinshed's *Chronicles of England, Scotland and Ireland*, first published in 1574, was a primary source of reference for a number of Shakespeare's plays, and *Macbeth* is no exception. The following extract from Holinshed's *Chronicles* demonstrates just how closely Shakespeare borrowed from his version of events:

"It fortuned as Makbeth and Banquho iournied towards Fores, where the king then laie, they went sporting by the waie togither without other company saue onelie themselues, passing thorough the woods and fields, when suddenlie in the middest of a laund, there met them three women in strange and wild apparell, resembling creatures of the elder world, whome when they attentiuelie beheld, woondering much at the sight, the first of them spake and said: All haile Makbeth, thane of Glammis (for he had latelie entered into that dignitie and office by the death of his father Sinell). The second of them said: Haile Makbeth thane of Cawder. But the third said: All haile Makbeth that heereafter shalt be king of Scotland.

Then Banquho: What manner of women (saith he) are you, that seeme so little fauourable vnto me, whereas to my fellow heere, besides high offices, ye assigne also the kingdome, appointing foorth nothing for me at all? Yes, (saith the first of them) we promise greater benefits vnto thee, than vnto him, for he shall reigne in deed, but with an vnluckie end: neither shall he leaue anie issue behind him to succeed in his place, where contrarilie thou in deed shalt not reigne at all, but of thee those shall be borne which shall gouern the Scotish kingdome by long order of continuall descent. Herewith the foresaid women vanished immediatlie out of their sight."

In those days, the Stuart Kings of Scotland (King James I was a Stuart) were believed to have descended from Banquo (this is unproven but may have some truth in it). The witches "predicted" a long line of kings and this is dealt with in the play verbally in Act I Scene III (page 15), and visually in Act IV Scene I (page 85) when Macbeth is shown a large number of kings in a line, that all bear a resemblance to Banquo. The "bloodline" is only made possible by Fleance escaping when his father is attacked. Holinshed describes how Walter Steward, the founder of the Stuart royal family, who married the daughter of Robert Bruce was a descendent of Fleance and therefore Banquo. This ancestral connection must have been behind a change that Shakespeare made to Holinshed's accounts, namely that in Holinshed, Banquo was an accomplice in Duncan's murder; to show an ancestor of the King to have acted unlawfully would have

been rather foolhardy on Shakespeare's part. Other pandering includes the reference to the English King (Edward the Confessor) having God-given powers to cure "the evil" in Act IV Scene III (page 99), also known as Scrofula. Edward was believed to have that power, and King James I revived the custom of sufferers being "touched" by the monarch as a cure for it.

But it is with his portrayal of the witches where Shakespeare really aimed to please the King. In his book, King James denounced witchcraft absolutely. It was his belief that witches were mostly women who had masculine features, typified by facial hair. They were in league with the devil, could summon up spirits, and could even curse images of people to control their destiny. These were early days in the understanding of witchcraft, and the very subject was a threat to King James' belief of divine right of kingship. In his world,

witchcraft was a devil-based display of evil that was an ever-present challenge to the sanctity of his God-given ruling. It is a general fear of witchcraft, then, that is the possible reason why neither Holinshed nor Shakespeare ever refer to the women as witches. In fact, the elements of witchcraft that exist in the play, particularly the spells and the appearance of Hecate, are now believed to be later additions, made by Thomas Middleton following on from his own play, "The Witch". The term only appears once, in Act I Scene III (page 12*) and even then it could be an insult being reported by the speaker.

Beyond the belief that it was written for the visit of the King of Denmark in 1606, a number of other elements point towards it being authored in that year. The Porter's ramblings in Act II Scene III (page 38*) make mention of equivocation:

"O, come in, equivocator", which is thought to refer to the verbal cunning displayed by Father Garnet, one of the Gunpowder Plot conspirators in his trial of 1606. Also that year, a ship called The Tiger returned to England after a terrible two year voyage – and that ship is named in Act I Scene III (page 12*). However, as the first printed version of the play didn't appear until the Folio printing in 1623, the true dating and authenticity of each of the parts of the play are difficult to establish. For certain, a version of the play was first performed at The Globe Theatre in April 1611.

The Scottish Play

Macbeth is steeped in superstition; so much so that actors consider it the height of bad luck to even utter the name, unless they are rehearsing it at the time. Often, people will make references to "The Bard's Play" or "The Scottish Play" simply to avoid saying the "M"-word. There are a number of theories about the origins of the "curse" of *Macbeth*:

- It is thought that the witches' incantations are taken from real rituals and are believed to cast actual spells on the players.
- Legend has it that in 1606, Hal Berridge, the boy playing Lady Macbeth (remember that all the parts, male and female, were played by males at the time) died backstage.
- Another gruesome legend reports how in 1672 an actor playing the part of Macbeth substituted a real dagger for the blunt stage one, and actually killed the actor playing King Duncan in full view of the audience.

The more rational explanations are easier to accept.

- The majority of the play takes place in darkly lit scenes, and this tended to lead to a lot of accidents backstage.
- Yet another theory is that because *Macbeth* is a short play, and is so well known, that theatre groups would perform the play when they were in some financial trouble. Of course, a single play is rarely enough to save an ailing company, and therefore the performance of *Macbeth* became associated with failure, misery, and being out of work.

Whether any of those reasons are true or not is open to much speculation; what is beyond any doubt is that the story of *Macbeth* is a powerful, timeless tale of ambition, of the evil that is embedded in ill-gotten gains, and a question that lies at the heart of life itself – are we all the subjects of fate and destiny? Or do we carve out our own existence on this planet?

Page Creation

In order to create three versions of the same book, the play is first adapted into three scripts: Original Text, Plain Text and Quick Text. While the degree of complexity changes for the dialogue in each script, the artwork remains the same for all three books.

On the left is a rough thumbnail sketch of page 73 created from the script (below). Once the rough sketch is approved it is redrawn as a clean finished pencil sketch (right).

HECATE BRIGHT GREEN EYES HER WORD BALLOON BLACK WITH RED GREEK TYPE FACE

ACT 3 – SCENE 5

249. Somewhere far beyond the light of the sun, the three Witches huddle. Strange weather and strange landscapes surround them. They sense the approach of Hecate, the Queen of Darkness and they're frightened.

250. BIG. Suddenly she's there! Hecate appears as a triple goddess, with three heads (women's in this frame, all identical, harsh-looking, but not ugly) and three bodies, standing back-to-back. She towers over the three Witches, piercing the gloom with her fierce stare. They cringe and make frightened animal noises.

	QUICK TEXT	PLAIN ENGLISH TEXT	ORIGINAL TEXT
WITCHES (2 & 3)	WHIMPER! WHINE!	WHIMPER! WHINE!	WHIMPER! WHINE!
1ST WITCH	Hecate…you look angry	Hecate! You look so angry	Why, how now, Hecate! you look angerly
HECATE	I am! You dared to meddle with Macbeth In riddles and affairs of death	Have I not reason, chats that you are, Impertinent and rash? How did you dare To trade and traffic with Macbeth, In riddles, and affairs of death;	Have I not reason, beldams as you are, Saucy, and overbold? How did you dare To trade and traffic with Macbeth, In riddles, and affairs of death;

251. BIGish. The Witches scuttle round Hecate like dogs round their master. Hecate's three heads metamorphose into the heads of a horse, a dog and a boar.

HECATE	You did it without me! And now I clearly see That all you've managed to do Is use him as he has used you.	And I, the mistress of your charms, The true instrument of all harms, Was never called to play my part, Or show the glory of our art? And, which is worse, all you have done Was only for a wayward son, Spiteful, and hateful; who, as others do, Wants all he can get and nought for you.	And I, the mistress of your charms, The close contriver of all harms, Was never call'd to bear my part, Or show the glory of our art? And, which is worse, all you have done Hath been but for a wayward son, Spiteful, and wrathful; who, as others do, Loves for his own ends, not for you.

From the pencil sketch an inked version of the same page is created (right).

Inking is not simply tracing over the pencil sketch, it is the process of using black ink to fill in the shaded areas and to add clarity, cohesion, depth and texture to the "pencils".

The "inks" give us the final outline which is checked for accuracy before being passed on to the colourist.

HECATE BRIGHT GREEN EYES HER WORD BALLOON BLACK WITH RED GREEK TYPE FACE

Adding colour brings the page and its characters to life.

Each character has a detailed character study drawn. This is useful for the artists to refer to and ensures continuity throughout the book.

Macbeth character study

The last stage of page creation is to add the speech bubbles and any sound effects.

Speech bubbles are created from the words in the script and are laid over the finished coloured artwork.

Three versions of lettering are produced for the three different versions of *Macbeth*. These are then saved as final artwork pages and compiled into separate books for printing.

Shakespeare Around the Globe

The Globe Theatre and Shakespeare

It is hard to appreciate today how theatres were actually a new idea in William Shakespeare's time. The very first theatre in Elizabethan London to only show plays, aptly called "The Theatre", was introduced by an entrepreneur by the name of James Burbage. In fact, "The Globe Theatre", possibly the most famous theatre of that era, was built from the timbers of "The Theatre". The landlord of "The Theatre" was Giles Allen, who was a Puritan that disapproved of theatrical entertainment. When he decided to enforce a huge rent increase in the winter of 1598, the theatre members dismantled the building piece by piece and shipped it across the Thames to Southwark for reassembly. Allen was powerless to do anything, as the company owned the wood - although he spent three years in court trying to sue the perpetrators!

The report of the dismantling party (written by Schoenbaum) says:

"ryotous... armed... with divers and manye unlawfull and offensive weapons... in verye ryotous outragious and forcyble manner and contrarye to the lawes of your highnes Realme... and there pulling breaking and throwing downe the sayd Theater in verye outragious violent and riotous sort to the great disturbance and terrefyeing not onlye of your subjectes... but of divers others of your majesties loving subjectes there neere inhabitinge."

William Shakespeare became a part owner of this new Globe Theatre in 1599. It was one of four major theatres in the area, along with the Swan, the Rose, and the Hope. The exact physical structure of the Globe is unknown, although scholars are fairly sure of some details through drawings from the period. The theatre itself was a closed structure with an open courtyard where the stage stood. Tiered galleries around the open area accommodated the wealthier patrons who could afford seats, and those of the lower classes - the "groundlings" - stood around the platform or 'thrust' stage during the performance of a play. The space under and behind the stage was used for special effects, storage and costume changes. Surprisingly, although the entire structure was not very big by modern standards, it is known to have accommodated fairly large crowds - as many as 3,000 people - during a single performance.

The Globe II

In 1613, the original Globe Theatre burned to the ground when a cannon shot during a performance of *Henry VIII* set fire to the thatched roof of the gallery. Undeterred, the company completed a new Globe (this time with a tiled roof) on the foundations of its predecessor. Opened in 1614, Shakespeare didn't write any new plays for this theatre. He retired to Stratford-Upon-Avon that year, and died two years later. Despite that, performances continued until 1642, when the Puritans closed down all theatres and places of entertainment. Two years later, the Puritans razed the building to the ground in order to build tenements upon the site. No more was to be seen of the Globe for 352 years.

Shakespeare's Globe

Led by the vision of the late Sam Wanamaker, work began on the construction of a new Globe in 1993, close to the site of the original theatre. It was completed three years later, and Queen Elizabeth II officially opened the New Globe Theatre on June 12th, 1997 with a production of *Henry V*.

The New Globe Theatre is as faithful a reproduction as possible to the Elizabethan theatre, given that the details of the original are only known from sketches of the time. The building can accommodate 1,500 people between the galleries and the "groundlings".

www.shakespeares-globe.org

AVAILABLE IN THREE TEXT VERSIONS

Macbeth:
The Graphic Novel
Original Text

ISBN:
978-1-906332-03-7

THE ENTIRE PLAY TRANSLATED INTO PLAIN ENGLISH!

Macbeth:
The Graphic Novel
Plain Text

ISBN:
978-1-906332-04-4

THE ENTIRE PLAY IN QUICK MODERN ENGLISH FOR A FAST-PACED READ!

THE ENTIRE SHAKESPEARE PLAY AS A GRAPHIC NOVEL!

Macbeth:
The Graphic Novel
Quick Text

ISBN:
978-1-906332-05-1

CHOOSE FROM ONE OF THREE TEXT VERSIONS, ALL USING THE SAME HIGH QUALITY ARTWORK:

Original Text

This is the full, original script - just as The Bard intended. This version is ideal for purists, students and for readers who want to experience the unaltered text; all of the text, all of the excitement!

Plain Text

We take the original script and "convert" it into modern English, verse-for-verse. If you've ever wanted to fully appreciate the works of Shakespeare, but find the original language rather cryptic, then this is the version for you!

Quick Text

We take the dialogue and reduce it to as few words as possible, but still retain the full essence of the story. This version allows readers to enter into and enjoy the stories quickly.

Shakespeare's plays in a choice of 3 text versions. Simply choose the text version to match your reading level.

Original Text — SHAKESPEARE'S ENTIRE PLAY AS A FULL-COLOUR GRAPHIC NOVEL!

Plain Text — THE ENTIRE PLAY TRANSLATED INTO PLAIN ENGLISH!

Quick Text — THE ENTIRE PLAY IN QUICK MODERN ENGLISH FOR A FAST-PACED READ!

A Midsummer Night's Dream: The Graphic Novel (William Shakespeare)

- Script Adaptation: John McDonald • Lettering: Jim Campbell
- Characters & Artwork: Jason Cardy & Kat Nicholson

144 Pages • £9.99

ISBN: 978-1-906332-89-1   ISBN: 978-1-906332-90-7   ISBN: 978-1-906332-91-4

Romeo & Juliet: The Graphic Novel (William Shakespeare)

- Script Adaptation: John McDonald • Linework: Will Volley
- Colours: Jim Devlin • Letters: Jim Campbell

168 Pages • £9.99

ISBN: 978-1-906332-19-8   ISBN: 978-1-906332-20-4   ISBN: 978-1-906332-21-1

The Tempest: The Graphic Novel (William Shakespeare)

- Script Adaptation: John McDonald • Pencils: Jon Haward
- Inks: Gary Erskine • Colours: & Letters: Nigel Dobbyn

144 Pages • £9.99

ISBN: 978-1-906332-29-7   ISBN: 978-1-906332-30-3   ISBN: 978-1-906332-31-0

Henry V: The Graphic Novel (William Shakespeare)

- Script Adaptation: John McDonald • Pencils: Neill Cameron • Inks: Bambos
- Colours: Jason Cardy & Kat Nicholson • Letters: Nigel Dobbyn

144 Pages • £9.99

ISBN: 978-1-906332-00-6   ISBN: 978-1-906332-01-3   ISBN: 978-1-906332-02-0

UR AWARD-WINNING RANGE

Classic Literature in a choice of 2 text versions. Simply choose the text version to match your reading level.

Original Text — THE CLASSIC NOVEL BROUGHT TO LIFE IN FULL COLOUR!

Quick Text — THE FULL STORY IN QUICK MODERN ENGLISH FOR A FAST-PACED READ!

Frankenstein: The Graphic Novel   (Mary Shelley)

- Script Adaptation: Jason Cobley • Linework: Declan Shalvey • Art Direction: Jon Haward
- Colours: Jason Cardy & Kat Nicholson • Letters: Terry Wiley

ISBN: 978-1-906332-15-0

ISBN: 978-1-906332-16-7

"Cursed be the hands that formed you!"

• 144 Pages • £9.99

Jane Eyre: The Graphic Novel   (Charlotte Brontë)

- Script Adaptation: Amy Corzine • Artwork: John M. Burns
- Letters: Terry Wiley

ISBN: 978-1-906332-06-8

ISBN: 978-1-906332-08-2

"I scorn your idea of love and the counterfeit sentiment you offer. And I scorn you when you offer it."

• 144 Pages • £9.99

A Christmas Carol: The Graphic Novel   (Charles Dickens)

- Script Adaptation: Seán Michael Wilson • Pencils: Mike Collins
- Inks: David Roach • Colours: James Offredi • Letters: Terry Wiley

ISBN: 978-1-906332-17-4

ISBN: 978-1-906332-18-1

"I will honour Christmas in my heart, and try to keep it all the year. I will live in the Past, the Present, and the Future."

• 160 Pages • £9.99

Great Expectations: The Graphic Novel   (Charles Dickens)

- Script Adaptation: Jen Green • Linework: John Stokes • Colouring: Digikore Studios Ltd
- Colour Finishing: Jason Cardy • Letters: Jim Campbell

ISBN: 978-1-906332-09-9

ISBN: 978-1-906332-11-2

"I never saw my father or my mother, and never saw any likeness of either of them."

• 160 Pages • £9.99